For Grandma and Grandpa

L. V.

First published 1991 by
Walker Books Ltd
87 Vauxhall Walk, London SE11 5HJ

Illustrations © 1991 Louise Voce

Printed and bound in Hong Kong by
South China Printing Co. (1988) Ltd

British Library Cataloguing in Publication Data
Lear, Edward, 1812-1888
The Owl and the Pussy cat.
I. Title II. Voce, Louise
821'.8

0-7445-1283-2

The Owl
and the
Pussy Cat

Written by
Edward Lear

Illustrated by
Louise Voce

WALKER BOOKS
LONDON

The Owl
and the Pussy cat
went to sea
In a beautiful
pea-green boat,

They took some honey,
and plenty of money,
Wrapped up in a
five-pound note.

The Owl looked up
to the stars above,
And sang
to a small guitar,

"O lovely Pussy!
O Pussy, my love,
What a beautiful
Pussy you are,
You are, you are!
What a beautiful
Pussy you are!"

Pussy said to the Owl,
"You elegant fowl!
How charmingly
sweet you sing!
O let us be married!
too long we have tarried:
But what shall we
do for a ring?"

They sailed
away, for a year
and a day,

To the land where
the Bong Tree grows,

And there in a wood
a Piggy-wig stood
With a ring
at the end of his nose,
His nose, his nose,
With a ring
at the end of his nose.

"Dear Pig,
are you willing
to sell for one shilling
Your ring?"
Said the Piggy, "I will."

So they took it away,
and were married
next day
By the Turkey
who lives on the hill.

They dined on mince,
and slices of quince,
Which they ate
with a runcible spoon;

And hand in hand,
on the edge of the sand,
They danced
By the light of the moon,
The moon, the moon,
They danced
by the light of the moon.